SEEDER STORIES

A COLLECTION OF BONUS SCENES FROM THE SEEDER WARS SERIES

J. HOUSER

Painted Wings Publishing

Note from the Author

I originally wrote these bonus scenes as giveaway incentives for preorders. Since future readers wouldn't have that same opportunity to experience these bonus stories, I wanted to give them the chance to enjoy the delicious tidbits that happen off-page to our favorite characters. I also wanted to offer the opportunity to have these accessible in one place, whether in print or ebook. As such, this is intended as a companion read to the Seeder Wars series, not to be read as a standalone novel.

To avoid spoilers, each section discloses the reading order at the very beginning. I hope you enjoy!

Sign up for my newsletter to be the first to know about upcoming publications, promotions, and bonus content at **JHouserWrites.com**

Table of Contents

Son & Soldier:
A Seeder Short Story

Can be read at any point in the series. A 'slice of life' story, written as an introduction to the Green Lands and green folk.

Almost-fifteen-year-old Evan wants nothing more than to be picked as one of the family protectors. Off in the human world, his twelve sisters' powers are about to come in. They'll need a teacher, a guide, and a protector. In the human world, Ivy assassins are always on the hunt for Seeder girls hidden in plain sight. Seeder girls just like his sisters.

Evan arrived late to the sports park, the one just down the lane from his house. He'd volunteered for extra guard duty at the Outer Wall that day. As usual, there hadn't been any enemy attacks, but he wanted to be prepared and well-trained.

A smile grew on his face as he approached the field, spotting eight of his eleven brothers sparring with other neighborhood boys. He broke into a sprint, moving energy to his arms and legs as he launched forward at the edge of the field, tackling a neighbor boy that had pinned down one of his brothers.

"Ugh." The boy shoved Evan off. "Jerk!"

"I'm the jerk?" Evan glanced back at his brother, who was perfectly fine. "I was just practicing. I imagined you were a leech. Lucky for you, I didn't pull out anything sharp."

The boy rolled his eyes. "You're not going to get selected. Stop dreaming." He stood up, brushing grass off of himself. "You'll meet your sisters someday, like all the rest of us." He stomped away with a huff.

Evan fought to hide a smile. *Sisters.* They were like unicorns—a myth, a legend. Millions of Seeders resided in the Green Lands. Not a single one of them was a girl under the age of fifteen. Imagining growing up with a sister was like imagining growing up with your father there to raise you.

But just like every other boy in this park, Evan had a father. They'd just never met. And he had sisters—twelve of them. While Evan would be excited to see them trickling home from the human world, he wanted nothing more than to be chosen as one of the boys in their family to go help out over there.

And that's what his jerk of a neighbor had so kindly reminded him of. Evan *hadn't* been chosen as their family's deep cover. That was Seth. Evan had worked *so* hard to learn everything needed to be chosen as their first protector to report for duty in the human world—just to be beat out by Seth. It left a bitter taste in Evan's mouth for months. But over time, his anger fueled his motivation to train harder, and Seth's presence was something he missed even more. Evan could now admit that he hadn't been far enough along with flying, learning to catch a breeze. Not at eight years old. And perhaps he hadn't even been as good as Seth had been in preparations for blending in with humans.

Three years after Seth left for the human world, rumors circulated amongst his brothers that their mom was ready to send the next boy. *This* time it would be Evan.

But again, it wasn't.

It wasn't like all of his brothers even wanted to go to the human world. Evan wrestled with his decision to pursue human education so intensively—maybe he'd just resign himself to guarding the border walls, or taking up a normal job at the local cotton farm.

That all sounded boring, less patriotic. He didn't want to settle.

"Pretty girls alert." One of his brothers, Derek, caught his attention, putting his arm around Evan's shoulders.

Evan chuckled. "Dream on." He knew it wouldn't lead anywhere, but it never hurt to admire as they walked by. The pair of girls giggled at the dozens of eyes on them. The guys that stood even half a chance approached. Evan knew with absolute certainty he *didn't* stand a chance, nor did his brothers. They were only fourteen.

When girls began returning to their ancestral lands, they could have their pick of the lot. Guys lined up in hopes of impressing the girls and getting a date. Evan promised himself he wouldn't be caught drooling, wouldn't be one of those guys who pounced on every chance to date a newly returned girl.

And if he was picked for protection duty like he hoped, he wouldn't be able to date for a few years, anyway. He could date a human girl, but it could never last, and would only be a distraction.

"Come on, Evan." Derek punched him in the arm. "Too tired from an extra shift on border patrol?"

Evan narrowed his eyes at the challenge. He extended his right arm's blade, a built-in weapon for Seeders, as well as part of what made it possible to fly. While the green blade, extending between his wrist and elbow, appeared menacing and could be lethal, he didn't flex to sharpen it. This was just sparring.

Derek grinned and extended both of his blades, moving them up to meet Evan's first strike.

After an extra hour of sparring at the park, Evan was beat. He moseyed down the lane to their family's lot. Before going to the kids' house in the back, he stopped by the main cottage.

Walking in the front door, he quickly spotted his mom sitting in the living room. She was fixated on a piece of paper, tears rolling down her cheeks.

Evan frowned. "Are you okay?"

"Of course, she's okay," a voice called from the kitchen.

Evan leaned to the side, not completely sure if he recognized the voice. It couldn't be…

"Those are happy tears," Seth said, stepping forward with a grin.

Evan's eyes grew wide. "Seth!" He lunged for his brother, pulling him into a tight hug. "Gosh, it's been so long!"

Seth released him after a minute. "Have you learned nothing from your training? Human teenage boys don't hug so much."

Evan rolled his eyes. "You're not with the humans. You're home."

Seth nodded with the tiniest smile. "Sometimes I almost forget what it's like to be here."

Evan glanced at his mom again. She sniffled and turned the paper over. Seth's visit meant news. He only made the trip once a year, to bring news from their dad. Evan desperately wanted to take a look at what his mom was poring over, but he knew he'd have to wait. Letters from their dad. Pictures and news of their sisters. Mom always took time poring over them in private, but then the boys would have a chance, and she deserved that privacy. She hadn't ever met her daughters, hadn't seen her husband in almost a decade and a half. She wasn't capable of visiting the human world anymore. And for his dad to leave his charges alone, even for a day, was the mark of a coward. Seeder fathers didn't risk their covers to visit loved ones back home in the Green Lands.

And it was all because of the Ivies—the leeches—the only other race in the Green Lands. The enemy that forced Seeders to raise their daughters in the human world in the first place, after poisoning

Seeder lands. The race that sent assassins to hunt down those girls in the human world.

Seth nudged Evan in the arm, gesturing with his head to the door. "Let's give her some space. I was going to go claim my old room."

Evan nodded, pondering. "Yeah, I'll meet you in a minute."

Seth shrugged. "Okay. Anyone else home?"

"Umm…" Evan was already lost in thought. "I think there's a couple back at the kids' house."

"Alright." Seth took off, heading out the front door.

Evan watched his mom a while longer. He wanted to be picked when the next son was called for duty. It wasn't just the allure of living with humans. It wasn't just for pride. It wasn't just for family. It was all of it. "Mom?"

She continued to read her letter. He sighed, walking toward the front door.

"Evan? Did you say something?"

He looked back. She wiped away her tears, her trance now broken.

"Well, I…" He hesitated. "I just … I want to go, when the next opportunity arises."

She gave him a soft smile. "I know, sweetie."

He bit his lip, nodding. "Yeah, well, I guess I'll see you later?"

She nodded with a brighter smile.

Stepping into the common room of the kids' house, Evan was greeted by a couple more brothers and an aunt, all surrounding Seth. Seth was donning his purple hair tips. Some of the Seeder powers were useful, a natural extension of who they were. Displaying your spiked purple hair … that was either a serious lack of control, or a stylistic choice. Evan grinned, knowing Seth was doing it just to enjoy the freedom to be himself. A human might see the change as a unique look, if Seth expended energy regularly to keep showing the spiked purple hair. If there were Ivy assassins in that human town, in that high school, it would be a dead giveaway that Seth was a Seeder.

Jarod, another brother, was in the shared kitchen, chopping fresh-picked kale and herbs from the garden. Seth's visit meant a big family meal. Evan knew he should help with the cooking, but he didn't want to waste a minute when he could be hearing stories from Seth.

Evan sat on the common room rug, facing Seth. "So, just here for the day? Or a couple days to recharge and make the journey back?"

Seth grinned. "I guess I forgot to tell you. I'm not just here to deliver news."

Evan's heart raced. "But you said it was good news. Do you suspect an Ivy network there?"

Seth shook his head. "We're fine. But I'm bringing someone back with me. Our first sister is showing the signs."

Evan's jaw dropped. He was completely floored. The first of his sisters was budding? Going through her bloom? Her powers were coming in. Her brothers would help her train. She'd be safe to return home. "So young?"

Seth shrugged. "We'll all be fifteen in a couple months. Mom was young when she went through hers."

Evan's mind raced. This was *huge* news. Girls usually began their bloom around the same age their mother had. Twelve girls would soon be finding out they weren't actually humans. They'd learn their heritage. They'd learn to wield their powers. They'd have to learn how to keep their true identities hidden. Desperation ached in Evan's heart. If he was overlooked this time… He now questioned every decision he'd been making. Did taking on extra border patrol duties make it seem like he had given up on his desire for protection detail? Or did it show his dedication, as he'd hoped it would?

Reminding himself he'd done all he could, Evan tried his best to push those concerns aside. He instead listened to Seth recount stories about their dad. About training sessions in secret. About his observations of their sisters. It reminded Evan of the countless evenings over the years that they'd all gathered around their mom, listening to her captivating stories about how she fell in love with their dad. About what it was like to grow up in the human world, and then face the decision to return home to the Green Lands. It was the adventure of a lifetime.

Eventually, boys filled the picnic tables nestled next to the jungle of a garden. Their mom and a couple of aunts and uncles joined them. As the matriarch, Evan's mom stood at the head before everyone dug in.

"We're all glad to have Seth back for a short visit." She smiled at him. "And yes, that means letters and pictures for everyone to see after dinner." She took a deep breath, standing tall. "I'm sure you've also heard someone will be joining Seth for duty." She scanned the group, making eye contact with those in the group more vocal about their desire to go.

Evan tried to play it cool, though he had a feeling his eyes would give away his hope. His fear. Would he be overlooked again?

"You know we don't take this decision lightly," his mom continued. "I'll be considering your interests in going, as well as speaking with your instructors. Remember that if you're not picked to go now, or at all—it doesn't mean I'm not proud of you."

Had that been specifically aimed at Evan? He really didn't think anyone else wanted it as much as he did. Or maybe his brothers were just better at hiding it. And maybe that was his problem. Maybe he cared too much. Or he wasn't good enough at concealing his feelings.

The next evening, Evan skipped out on extra sparring practice. It was foolish. He should've been out there demonstrating what he was made of. Showing why he was worthy of being chosen.

Instead, he sat alone in the cottage living room, poring over the letters again and taking in the faces of his sisters. Seth and their dad had collected pictures from each of the host families. These girls were so foreign. Such a mystery. He smiled at a picture of three of them, having been raised as triplets. All of these girls were strangers. To him. To his mom. And even to themselves.

"Hi, sweetheart." His mom's voice claimed his focus.

He set down the photo he was holding. "Hey."

She frowned. "How are you doing?"

He looked down. "Fine."

She sat down with a sigh. "You want to go."

Looking up, he met her gaze. "Of course, I do."

She crossed her arms. "Why?"

He shifted, barely able to scrape together the plea he'd given on a dozen separate occasions. "You know why. I want to meet Dad. And my sisters."

She slowly nodded. "But they'll all be back in two or three years now. Would it be so bad to wait?"

"It's not just that." He struggled, wishing he were more articulate. "I want to make a difference. I want to help."

She cocked her head to the side. "We all contribute. We learn and teach. We cook and clean. We patrol the borders and go to the human world. Just because something's not your first choice, doesn't mean it's not worthwhile."

He huffed. "I know. Is this your way of saying I should stop trying?"

She shook her head. "I love your determination. I just want to make sure you fully understand what you're signing up for. You don't have to worry about human discovery here. Or Ivy assassins. It's dangerous over there."

Evan pursed his lips. "I know. I understand what I'd be signing up for."

She stared at him for an uncomfortable amount of time. "It's hard for a mother to choose. Which son she'll be putting in danger.

Which one will be the best to help keep the others safe. It's a lot to ask of a fourteen-year-old." She paused. "But you've worked hard. And I think you're up to the challenge."

His eyes grew wide, his heart filling with hope. "I'm going?"

She smiled. "Yes."

He hopped up and she rose to meet him. Evan gave her a tight squeeze, absolutely giddy.

He stepped back, straightening himself out and clearing his throat. *You can't be giddy. Human teenage boys don't hug all the time, and they certainly aren't giddy.*

"Thank you," he said.

She gave him another smile, though it didn't reach her eyes. "No. Thank you. I'm going to miss you every day you're gone." She twisted her mouth, unsuccessfully fighting back tears. "Get them all home safe."

"I will."

That night, Evan tidied up his little room, and made sure his laundry was clean and put away. He'd be taking with him the clothes on his back and letters in his pockets—that was all. He struggled to sleep, thinking of the human world. All the amazing stories he'd heard. Girls. Sisters. His dad. Electronics. It was finally happening.

The next morning, Evan was greeted by the brothers he'd be leaving behind. Most that hadn't been chosen hid their disappointment well. He tried not to appear too excited, not wanting to rub it in. And for all he knew, it would be two or three years before he'd see them all again. Only one son was needed to deliver news, and it would usually be Seth. His cover was so well established that no one would question him taking off for a couple of days to 'go visit family.'

After a final round of hugs, Evan's mom divvied up letters for them to exchange. Evan tucked the precious cargo in his pocket and joined Seth, walking down the dirt lane to their takeoff point.

Evan's stomach was in knots. He was leaving home. He was walking into the lion's den. Not that he'd ever seen a lion in real life—they didn't exist in the Green Lands. But he'd been taught what they were. All of the knowledge he'd taken in during his years of training flooded into his mind. *Can't just walk into the lane … I mean street. You have to be careful to look around, because the car-things could run you over. They eat meat.* He shivered. That was so weird to imagine—consuming flesh. But apparently bacon was worth trying. *I'll give it a go.*

"How bad are the human schools?" Evan asked, kicking a rock from his path.

Seth chuckled. "They're easier in some ways. Less physical exertion. Then again, they're more boring without sparring practice." A smile crept up on his face. "And then there's the girls…"

Evan scoffed. "*Human* girls."

He already knew he wouldn't have time to date human girls, unless his dad's orders allowed or expected it for his cover. But he didn't need to waste his time with some needy girl while he should be focusing on his sisters. From a distance, he'd ensure they went through their blooming smoothly, undetected. He'd watch for signs of Ivy assassins—especially the creeps that might try to date his sisters. Ivies rarely sent female assassins, so they really just had to worry about the guys. And what better way to take down a Seeder family network, than to get close to a Seeder girl?

Seth shrugged. "Human girls are as pretty as any of ours. But remember not to gawk. It's weird, seeing an even gender ratio."

Evan shook his head. "I know. I can blend in. I'll pretend like it's normal."

"I'm just saying … it's a culture shock. You've got to act like being in a car is something you've done every day of your life."

Evan huffed. "I know. I know all of this."

Seth turned, putting a hand on Evan's shoulder. "I know. I'm just saying, it takes a lot of getting used to."

Reaching the clearing most of the Seeders in this part of their village used for takeoff, they stopped. Evan rubbed his hands together, the conflict of emotions assaulting him. *I can do this.*

Seth took a deep breath. "We'll go to safehouse B first." He looked Evan over. "You'll change clothes there. Then we only have three days. I'll be teaching you things you're not able to really do over here. You'll learn to use a cell phone. And how to play video games."

Evan nodded. He'd heard those were fun. Human electronics didn't function properly with the ambient energy in the Green Lands.

"Seeder given names are only to be used amongst the family network. Use their human names out in the open."

Evan nodded again, the tension building inside him.

"Everything's set up at your host family's house. Your cover is already established. The number one thing is to *blend in*. This isn't just sparring. If all goes well, you'll never actually have to fight anyone. This is about observing. Learning and teaching. If you see even the tiniest glimmer of green in one of our sisters' eyes—report to me or Dad immediately."

"Yeah. Got it." Evan's heart was racing. There would be so much to juggle.

Seth grinned. "But don't forget to have a *little* fun. Dad said I could date a girl to help with my cover. Her name's Hailey. Turns out kissing is pretty awesome."

Evan smirked. "Way to take one for the team."

They turned, standing side by side, ready to go. Evan took a deep breath; this would be the last time he'd stand on Green Lands soil in a long time. He felt the unique energy of the realm flowing within him. He knew he'd miss it. He'd miss a lot. But he had a job to do.

Evan and Seth sprinted across the grass, leaping forward and transforming completely. Spiked purple hair, green arm blades extended, roots exposed—all of it. They balanced their energy, catching a breeze, like they'd done a thousand times before. Evan looked ahead, following Seth's lead. It would be hours of flight between their village and the rifting space. Then hours more before arriving at the safe house. It would be exhausting. And it would be worth it.

Evan beamed, seeing his dream finally fulfilled. His dad. His sisters.

He gulped.

And possibly, Ivy assassins.

The Return & Question

**Best when read between Seeder Shadow Wars &
Trouble in the Green Lands**

Saff peered into the windows of the central marketplace found in her home village of South Fortinda. It was a bit of a windy day, and the central shopping lane was muddy from the morning's showers, but she loved the smell of the Green Lands after it rained. And she desperately needed a distraction.

"Now *that* is a cute hair clip," Dahlia said as they slowed to look at a vendor selling all sorts of ribbons and accessories.

Tabatha grinned at Saff. Dahlia was still the frillier of the three of them. Possibly of all twelve of the girls in their family.

"Definitely cute. But Murial asked for us to bring home lemons." Saff raised an eyebrow and a basket of apples. Their primary purpose in this excursion was for trade.

Dahlia met her challenge with a smirk. "With how crazy you've been acting all week, I'd think you'd be grateful to spend all day shopping."

Saff couldn't help but blush. "I don't know what you're talking about." She averted her gaze and continued walking.

"Uh-huh…" Dahlia replied playfully, and Tabatha giggled.

Biting her lip, Saff tried her best to ignore them. They were both right. She'd been pacing, and sleepless, and excited, and terrified for days. Devin was expected to return home this week. Finally.

It had been almost a year since Saff had left the human world, since she'd seen Devin. Luckily, she'd gotten a few letters from him, courtesy of several of her brothers—and his—who had trickled home before him. But his last sister had finally bloomed and was fully trained, set to catch a breeze and rift home any day now. Saff had hardly even eaten that week with her stomach in knots. They'd only dated a few months, and now they'd been apart, in completely different realms, for more than twice as long. What if they didn't feel the same way about each other once he got back?

Taking a deep breath, Saff tried to stop obsessing. He'd return safely. They'd see how things went. Stressing over it all did her no good.

"So…" Tabatha linked her arm through Saff's. "What are your plans for tonight?"

Saff smiled. "Ben and I talked about going out to Glass Lake and skipping rocks." It was one of their favorite brother-sister hangouts. They would just go and chat, and he would identify flora and fauna for her. Parts of her surroundings were familiar— butterflies or apple trees just like in the human world—but sometimes there were things she didn't recognize, and she genuinely didn't know if they were from the human world and she just hadn't ever seen them over there, or if they were exclusively found in the Green Lands.

"Hmm. Mind if I tag along?" Tabatha asked.

Saff nudged her. "Of course not."

They continued their stroll, passing carts piled high with rhubarb, onions, several kinds of melons, and so much more. Little boys ran through the streets, sometimes being chased and scolded by an aunt, sometimes catching a breeze overhead. Seeder life was interesting.

"Oooh, I was hungry!" A large hand grabbed an apple from Saff's basket.

She spun to see Ben, right as he crunched into the crisp apple. "Excuse you. Mom wanted us to swap that. Not eat it."

Ben beamed, chewing away.

Saff just rolled her eyes.

"Saff said we're headed out to Glass Lake tonight?" Tabatha said.

Ben wrinkled his nose and finished his bite. "Nah. Well… Heather and I are going, and you can join if you want. But Saff's not invited anymore." His lips spread into a mischievous grin.

Saff's jaw dropped. "Why? You're an apple thief, and I'm suddenly disinvited to hang out because I called you out on it?"

He shook his head. "Nah." He took another huge bite of apple. "I just figure you'll be busy."

Furrowing her brow, Saff tried to think of anything she might have forgotten. But she didn't have any classes or trainings or other obligations she could remember.

Tabatha took in a sharp breath. "Saff."

"What?"

Ben cleared his throat, still grinning, then nodded at a figure standing across the lane.

Saff's heart stopped, as did her ability to breathe, as she spotted Devin. He leaned against a tree, crossing his arms, his lips curved in a gentle smile. Saff shoved the basket of apples into Ben's arms and ran across the lane.

Without hesitation, Devin opened his arms, and she launched herself into them. All of her pent-up nerves washed away in his embrace. *This* was the last thing she'd needed to feel fully at home. Devin was what made it complete.

"I missed you," he whispered, squeezing her even tighter.

"You too. But you're really home. Safe and sound."

He released her, but held her hands between them. They studied each other. He'd grown a little, and was somehow even cuter.

"Ben said…" he started. "Well, when you left you said… Just, you know. That you and I…"

She gazed into his deep-brown eyes. "I said I'd wait for you, and I did."

His smile widened.

Her heart was racing, but he still hesitated. She bit her lip. "Why aren't you kissing me right now?"

Without skipping a beat, he leaned in and did just that. Starting with a couple of short, sweet kisses, he soon pulled her in tight, laying a proper reunion kiss on her. It was a busy lane, and three of her siblings were watching, but it didn't matter.

And then Tabatha started clapping and cheering for them, and Saff had to step back and laugh. Tabatha had always been a dork that Saff could count on.

With Devin's arm wrapped around her, they approached her siblings.

"So, Saff, did you still want to hang out with me tonight?" Ben casually asked, before taking another bite of his apple.

She grinned in response. "I was disinvited, so I guess I'll have to figure out some other plans, won't I?"

Months later, Saff laid down a picnic blanket while Devin filled their water canteens from a nearby stream. She loved this park—it was one of their favorites, a little out of the way and less trafficked. Pulling the picnic basket onto the blanket, she sat, crossing her legs.

"Here you go." Devin handed her some water, joining her on the blanket.

Saff took a swig. "Thanks." As she went to open the basket, Devin stopped her, moving it just out of reach.

"I, uh … just wanted to talk a minute," he said.

She tilted her head to the side. "Okay." She hid a smile, knowing full well why he had picked this day to go on a special picnic. It was the two-year anniversary of their first kiss.

"Well, I just thought, you know. Well… I love you." He cleared his throat.

She smiled at his obvious anxiety. "I love you, too."

"Yeah. I love you, too." He shook his head. "I said that already. I just, um, well, happy anniversary."

She searched his face, knowing he wasn't one to stutter without something more to say than a simple 'happy anniversary.' "You too."

A breeze rustled the leaves on the tree above them, and she was brought back to the day he'd returned home. They'd come to this park that night. Their lips would have been raw if she hadn't been able to heal them as they'd kissed.

Reaching for his pocket, Devin confirmed her suspicions. His hands shook as he pulled out a ring. A beautiful diamond ring. His eyes focused on hers. "Build a life with me. Marry me."

She gave him a soft smile. "You're sure that's what you want?"

He furrowed his brow. "Of course it is."

She slowly, pensively nodded.

He looked into her eyes with desperation. "Most girls say yes or no at this point."

Grinning wide, she reached into her own pocket, pulling out her own ring. It was an intricately carved dark wooden ring she'd bartered for with an elderly craftsman in their village.

Devin's eyes darted between her face and the ring. "You got me one?"

Saff sighed. "I pay attention in culture classes. I'd get A's in them if they were graded that way. I know it's Seeder tradition for the woman to ask. You take on my family sash at the ceremony—I should be the one asking."

He cocked his head, smiling. "Come on. Most people still do the traditional ceremonies, but hardly anyone has the girl ask anymore. All of you come back with a human mindset about the guy asking."

She bit her lip in thought. This had become her home. Her people. "I think heritage is important. I love it here. As much as I love you. So, yes. I'll marry you, if you'll marry me."

His smile widened, until he looked down at the ring he'd gotten her. It was obviously a human design, nothing like Seeder jewelry. "I should have known that. I can get you something different."

She shook her head. "When did you even get it for me?"

His face turned pink as he ran a finger over the diamond. "Not long after you left. I guess it gave me something to look forward to, hoping you were waiting for me."

If he'd really bought it for her right after she'd left, that meant he'd been holding onto it for well over a year already. Her heart melted at his sweetness. "Then I love it even more."

He looked up, beaming. "You're sure?"

Nodding, she leaned in for a kiss. After pulling back, they exchanged rings. She instantly loved the feeling of it on her hand.

"Okay, then," he said with a sigh and a perma-smile. "Now the question is when. Obviously, spring is pretty popular, but that doesn't give us a lot of time to prepare."

With spring being the best time for female Seeders to make their yearly journey to the human world, it was common for those getting married to do it then. They could have a ceremony with human family and friends, and then a second ceremony back in the Green Lands.

Saff shrugged. "I don't need some huge to-do. You. Me. It's not like we don't have family nearby. When do *you* want to have the ceremony?"

His eyes roamed over her body, his mouth forming a mischievous grin. "Yesterday."

She smirked, leaning back on her elbows. "If we were married yesterday, we'd be doing *scandalous* things right now."

Devin inched forward, kneeling next to her. He bent down, caressing her neck with his lips. "They're not scandalous once you're married." He reached for her sides, tickling her.

Saff giggled and squirmed, shifting energy into her arms and legs to pin him down. She scrunched her nose. "No tickling!"

He grinned with defiance. "So, what will it be? What day are we aiming for?"

She sighed. "Would you hate it if we did spring?"

He shook his head with a soft smile. "I'd wait forever for you. I can manage spring."

She grinned back, letting his arms go but staying on top of him. "Forever? Then maybe we should push it back a couple years."

Narrowing his eyes, he moved his hands to her waist and hooked his fingers through the loops of her human-crafted jeans. "You think you are *sooo* funny."

She bit her lip.

"If you want spring, I vote first day of spring," he continued.

She raised her eyebrows in disbelief. "On sprout reveal day?"

"Fine." He playfully stuck out his tongue. "The week after?"

She nodded. "Sounds like a plan." She looked down at his shirt more pensively. "You're still thinking you want a clutch?"

"I do. I thought you did, too."

"I think I do." She ran her fingertips over the fabric of his shirt. "Kind of a huge decision to make, though."

He frowned. "But it's years before that's even an option. And if we decided to not have one in the end, I'd still have you. And be the luckiest husband and uncle in the world."

She swallowed hard, having heard her Seeder parents' love story and knowing how difficult it had been for them to make the decision to have kids. The Seeder way of family life was far from easy.

Saff drew a deep breath. "You. Me. Marriage. Spring. Then forever. We'll sort out the in-between as it comes."

He gave her a dimpled smile.

Saff's stomach growled and she chuckled. "Now, about that picnic basket. I'm starving."

Devin kept his hands on her waist as she straddled him. "I vote we start with some dessert."

She grinned, but halted her approach when she spotted a mother walking by with her dozen little boys. Some of the boys gawked; the mother's disapproving glance was obvious. Saff cleared her throat and removed Devin's hands, getting off of him with a blush. "Maybe a little more of that later."

Sitting up and following Saff's gaze, Devin realized the cause of her behavior change, and smiled and waved at the little boys. "Maybe we should dig into that basket after all." He pulled the basket open. "And let's talk about what we want in a cottage together."

Just the idea of sharing a cottage almost made her want to change her mind and move up the wedding. But they'd been this patient; they could wait a few more months. As Devin pulled item after item out of the picnic basket, she watched him with admiration.

This was what it meant to have it all.

Kaylah's Chronicles

**Best when read between Trouble in the Green Lands &
Unitas: Trio**

Kaylah lay in bed staring at her ceiling, trying to shake the fresh memory of panic, muffled screaming, and blood. *Lots* of blood. She slid a hand to her stomach, now queasy. The panic had been hers. Well, hers, Guillen's, and the teenage boy's just before she'd murdered him. The muffled screaming and blood had all been his.

Closing her eyes, she slowly inhaled, then let it go. It didn't work, though she hadn't really expected it to. There was no turning back at this point. It wasn't tantrums and political posturing. She'd officially risen to the level of treason and rebellion. *No.* She swallowed hard. *Words matter. It's revolution. It's reform. It's change.*

Her phone chimed. <Doing anything fun today?>

Kaylah frowned, not responding right away. It was her day to be available to occupy Rachel. But she didn't have it in her. She was too exhausted to spend time with Rachel. Not that Rachel herself was exhausting. Kaylah loved her like the best friend she was. But all of the lies were hard to keep track of, especially when compounded by the lies the royal family wasn't even privy to.

Sighing, Kaylah responded. <Got plans. Fun, though? Not so much :P What about you?> The truth was generally easiest, though ambiguity never hurt.

<Froyo with mom, just figured I'd see if you wanted to hang out.>

<Sounds like fun. Rain check?> Kaylah rolled her eyes. 'Rob' was 'out of town' for 'work,' anyway, and 'David' was 'hanging out with the guys.' They were both visiting the Green Lands—Rachel didn't need to be babysat today to be kept from walking in on some secret meeting.

<Rain check works for me. The offer stands if you end up ditching your other plans!>

Kaylah smiled. How could someone partially raised by a monster like her Uncle Nuren be so sweet and innocent? But she knew that answer. Rachel's human mom, Samantha, was really nice. And Kaylah's uncle had been forced to be kind, otherwise Samantha would have left him long ago, cutting off this experiment and opportunity.

Allowing her phone to drop by her side, Kaylah closed her eyes, taking a couple more deep breaths. She'd known she had been dancing with danger, and that taking a life might become necessary. She just hadn't really anticipated how it would feel. Sure, her mother had ordered people to their deaths, but had never actually done the dirty work of killing someone. At least not that Kaylah knew about.

Abruptly sitting up and rubbing her face, Kaylah let out a frustrated grunt. She needed a distraction. Something happy. Something without strings attached.

A soft knock sounded at her bedroom door.

"Come in."

Ginger appeared with a cheery smile. "How are you doing? Any thoughts on lunch and dinner today?" She paused. "Are you feeling alright? You haven't left your room all morning."

Forcing a smile, Kaylah had no choice but to lie. She wasn't ready to bring Ginger and Nathan into her plans yet. She loved them, but wasn't fully convinced their loyalty could be won. *Full* loyalty. The kind that was severed from her parents, their employers, their queen and king. "I'm fine. I think I'm going to go for a drive and just grab a bite while out. I'll let you know about dinner?"

"Sure thing. Stay in touch and reach out if you need us."

Kaylah swallowed. "Thanks. Will do." The moment Ginger shut the door, Kaylah knew she needed to get up and get out or she would stay in that bedroom for the rest of the day. Tucking her cell into her jeans, she grabbed her keys and left the house.

She was still not sure where she was headed. She'd told Rachel that she had plans. The truth was more that she had plans to *make* plans… Traffic was bustling, and once Kaylah left the busier streets, she happily replaced the crowded but smooth asphalt with the calming quiet isolation of an unpaved road. A large sign ahead brought a genuine smile to her face. She instantly knew what her afternoon was going to look like—the local animal shelter.

Taking a right, the car jostled her a bit with each dip in the dirt path. She'd desperately wanted a puppy or kitten when she was a little girl and had been brought to this realm to 'study humans.' They wouldn't allow her to have one. She had too much to do, to study, to learn. Kaylah frowned, feeling guilty for not inviting Rachel along. Rachel had wanted a pet, too. *Stupid Nuren.* He'd lied and said he was allergic because he didn't want one around. Rachel had been allowed a goldfish as a little girl. After it died, she'd never replaced Mr. Bubbles. Pulling into the shelter's gravel parking lot, where only three other cars sat parked, Kaylah turned off the car and rested her forehead on the steering wheel. Maybe she *should* invite Rachel—she would enjoy it.

Feeling as though she might die of old age before deciding, Kaylah sat up straight and let the idea go. She couldn't be fake with Rachel today, not in person.

This would actually be Kaylah's first time at the shelter, though she'd looked it up before and had considered swinging by. She nervously tucked her hands into her pockets, unsure of what the rules were as she approached the front desk. Muted barks belted out from another room, and a large cage sat behind the receptionist's desk. A tropical bird of some sort, missing several feathers, rested on its perch, eyeing her on her approach. Under the cage swung a label: "My name is Penny."

"Hi, how can I help you?" a woman, likely in her twenties, asked from behind the counter.

"Yeah, I was just wondering if you allow people to volunteer. Like … could I walk a dog today or something?"

The woman smiled. "Sure can. We have regular volunteers if you're interested in doing more, but if you'd just like to give one some fresh air outside, I can get you set up."

Kaylah nodded with a smile of her own. "Yeah, I'd love to. I don't know that I could make a long-term commitment, though."

Waving a dismissive hand in the air, the woman left her station and ushered Kaylah to a hallway. "No problem. Whichever little furry friend you walk today will appreciate the gesture, even if it's only this once."

They first passed by the cat rooms; they were in kennels visible through windows flanking the hallway. Rachel was more of a cat person. Kaylah liked dogs better. The noisy barks had grown louder as she walked down the hallway, but the sound doubled once the employee opened the door to the dog kennels. Kaylah instantly frowned, following the woman in. She'd come here to be happy with cute creatures, and hadn't expected to see them lined up in chain-link prisons. Kaylah's mind turned to Guillen, to the Seeders, to all of the other injustices out there. What had they done to deserve this?

"Do any of these dogs on the right interest you?" the woman asked.

Kaylah took a few steps, surveying the captives. An overgrown black beast barked at her, jumping against the chain-link. A scrawny little thing was curled into a ball, shaking in the back of another kennel. In the next, a wiener dog with wiry fur scratched itself, then licked its privates.

Catching her eye from a kennel on the left was a beautiful medium-sized grey dog, eagerly wagging its tail and letting out a couple of excited barks. She didn't know breeds that well, but she thought it might be a pit bull or something related to that. "Can I walk that one?"

"No, sorry. Only these on this side."

Disappointed, Kaylah turned back and picked the wiener dog. The woman set her up with a leash and guided Kaylah outside to the walking area. More chain-link fences, only four feet tall out here, edged the grass yard, also separating the yard into a few different sections. To the right, a couple and a small child were fawning over a puppy. After getting more instructions on policies and poop bags, Kaylah was all set.

The little dog happily plodded along, stopping randomly now and then to sniff and mark where another dog had likely left its calling card recently. It wobbled a smidge, perhaps a bit too round. One footstep after another, she wondered about the dog's history and how old it was—some of its hairs were randomly white.

This couldn't compare to the warmth of the energy in the Green Lands, but it almost allowed her to leave a fraction of her worries behind, on a nice day with a little dog.

After a few minutes lost in thought, Kaylah spotted another person entering the area, on the other side of one of the fences. Clicking the gate behind him, a tall blond held tight to a leash, walking the very dog she'd wanted to walk in the first place.

Hmm… She was instantly frustrated that she'd been denied. If she were back home in her kingdom, she would never have been denied this kind of request. Gently coaxing her dog to the fence, she took another glance at the dog on the other side. Yep. It was the one she'd wanted to walk.

"Hi," she said.

The blond turned his attention to her, as did his dog—it yanked on the leash and barked at the one she had been walking. "Hi. Can I help you?"

"I just…" She hesitated, not really sure what she'd planned on saying. "I wanted to walk him, but the lady told me no."

"Sorry. Not just anyone can handle this beast," he said casually, almost even playfully.

Kaylah eyed this guy. He wore dark jeans and a button-up shirt. He was just a pretty boy. His dog pulled on its leash again and her eyes rested on the guy's flexed bicep. Annoyance flared up inside her. A pretty-boy human thinking he was something special, thinking he was so much better and more capable because he was a guy, because he was stronger? If he only knew that she was a princess, a princess with powers, that could manipulate Ivy energy within her body. Having been to the Green Lands so recently, she could easily be stronger than this guy, without even using her vines or poison.

"What? I'm not capable of handling it because…?" She raised her eyebrows. "Because I don't have your bulging biceps? I'm strong enough to handle a bigger, rougher dog."

He instantly grinned, and then laughed. He actually *laughed* at her.

"Never mind. I'm not wasting my time talking to a jerk." She turned to head away. She'd come to relax, not to be mocked.

"Hold on," he said.

She turned to find him still grinning. She narrowed her eyes. "What?"

"I'm not a jerk."

She scoffed. "Could have fooled me."

"You want to know why I can handle this dog and you can't?"

Crossing her arms, she didn't answer, only tilting her head a smidge in response.

"Just…" He pointed at his upper arm. "I find it funny that you noticed my bulging biceps, but not," he drew his finger to his chest, a mere two or three inches over, landing on a metal name badge, "this?"

Kaylah pressed her lips together, reading the name badge. *Eric. Volunteer.* "Oh."

Eric cleared his throat, still sporting a slight smirk. "It has nothing to do with how strong you are. This dog just came in today. If you're not an employee or a trained volunteer, you're not allowed to work with a new animal until its temperament has been proven."

Biting her lip, she nodded. Her posture relaxed as she uncrossed her arms and slid her free hand into her pants pocket. "I just thought maybe it was a breed thing, or?"

Eric wrinkled his nose, changing hands for the leash. "We try not to be breedist."

"Breedist?" She lifted an eyebrow. "Is that an actual word?"

He gave her a handsome smile. "Probably not."

"Right… Well…" Still embarrassed about not having noticed his name tag and for jumping to conclusions, she was ready to move on.

"I'm Eric, though I guess you've figured that out by now." He extended his hand over the chain-link. "What's your name?"

She met his hand, shaking it. "Meg." Her alias was second nature by now, though it still killed her inside each time she had to introduce herself that way.

After releasing her hand, he reached down and scratched his dog's head. "So, if you wanted to walk this guy, are you looking to adopt a bigger dog?"

Kaylah spared a glance at her own dog, which was currently sniffing and marking the fence. "I'd probably be happy with any type of dog, to be honest. But I'm not looking to adopt right now. I'm not allowed."

"Hmm. Against … college dorm room rules this fall?"

She hid a smile at his possible fishing. School had just released for the year. "I'll be a senior in high school."

He smiled. "Me too. Which school?"

"Lincoln. You?"

He furrowed his brow, his smile growing. "Really? Me too. Are you new?"

"No. You?" For a split second, she was a little nervous at the prospect of a new male student, but that was such a tiny concern that it was practically a nonissue. Even *if* he were a new Seeder brother of Rachel's, it wasn't like he'd suspect a female Ivy assassin, or the crown princess. And, quite frankly, none of them would be wasting time volunteering here, away from sisters and crowds.

"Nope." Eric shook his head. "I've been here since the eighth grade."

They chatted for several minutes about the most popular kids and teachers. About how Mr. Tate was the funniest history teacher, how Mrs. Anderson made math even less enjoyable, and how the student body president had gotten into some sort of college admissions scandal. Kaylah found herself smiling, easily conversing with him, and even laughing as they walked up and down the fence length a couple of times.

"You said you're not allowed a dog right now. Is that—" He stopped. "Watch out for that—"

She didn't need him to finish the sentence as her sneaker came down into a squishy pile. Closing her eyes, she took a deep breath before glancing down. "That's so awesome."

Eric frowned. "Sorry, should have spotted it sooner."

"No. It's par for the course lately." She sighed, considering her options to scrape off the dog poop.

"Let me go grab some bags." He left, his dog in tow, grabbing a couple of bags and bringing them back.

Kaylah scraped off as much poop as she could into the bags, not able to get into the tread grooves.

"You said this is par for the course?" he asked, watching. "Stepping in a lot of dog poop lately?"

She quietly chuckled, turning a bag inside out and tying it up. "More like it's been a few crappy days."

"Sorry to hear that." His voice was sweet. "Maybe you need something fun to cheer you up. Do you have any plans tonight?"

She threw a quick glance down at her shoe. "Other than burning my shoes?"

Laughing, he leaned against the fence. "I know you said you're too busy for the volunteer program, but if you're not too busy tonight… I'm out of here in a couple hours…"

A smile grew on her face. "What do you have in mind?"

"Unless you'd prefer something else, I was thinking just basic dinner and a movie?"

She bit her lip, looking into his eyes. He was undeniably cute and friendly, but she shouldn't be wasting time on a human with everything else she had going on.

Then again… It could potentially save her from having to date more suitors sent by her parents. "That sounds like fun."

Now sporting fresh new shoes, Kaylah stood in front of the mirror in her bedroom, glad to have something to look forward to. She was actually surprised to find herself giddy about this date. She'd gone on plenty of dates, but very few she'd looked forward to. She recognized Ginger's soft knock on her door. "Come in."

"Your date is here," Ginger said, casually leaning against the doorframe. "Taking a breather from your parents' menu?"

Kaylah slid a necklace over her head. "You could say that."

"Have you approved him with your uncle?"

Kaylah gritted her teeth, trying to hide her annoyance. "I just met Eric today, and since my uncle's back home, I suppose I need your approval on this one." She arched an eyebrow.

Ginger pursed her lips. "I know you dislike all of the rules. But Nathan and I are here to keep you safe. If he hasn't been properly vetted…"

"Please," Kaylah whispered with a heavy heart. "He's already here. You know I can take care of myself. Can you please trust my judgment on this one?"

Approaching and resting her hands on Kaylah's arms, Ginger frowned. "I trust your judgment. And you know we want you to be happy, right?"

Kaylah hesitantly nodded.

"Enjoy your date. Be careful."

"Thanks!" Kaylah beamed, pulling Ginger into a hug.

Grabbing her purse, Kaylah made her way to the living room, where Nathan was chatting with Eric. She'd almost forgotten how cute he was. Once he spotted her, he also smiled.

"I'm all set," she announced, sliding her hands into her back jeans pockets.

"Great." Eric stood, nodding at Nathan. "It was nice to meet you."

After they got into Eric's car and turned down the music, there was a moment of awkward silence.

"How was the rest of your time at the shelter?" she asked.

He shifted gears. "Good. Always is."

She adjusted her air conditioner vent. "I bet it's a good place to pick up chicks."

He laughed. "Not really. But I don't always have pretty girls objectifying me, so you know, there's that."

Kaylah scoffed. "Objectifying you?"

Grinning, he didn't look away from the road. "Was it my bulky…? No, wait, *bulging* biceps." He threw her a playful glance.

Her cheeks warmed. "Well, that happened…"

Eric cleared his throat. "You look great."

She'd only added the necklace and changed her shoes. "Thanks, I wanted to feel like a real princess. If I learned one thing from Cinderella, it's that a pair of new shoes can do a lot for you."

Eric chuckled.

· ·🦋· ·

After hours of dinner, a movie, and ice cream and chatting, they ended the night on Kaylah's front porch.

"I had a lot of fun," Eric said.

Kaylah smiled softly. "Me too." And she genuinely had. She'd forgotten the lies, the pressure, the rules, the murder. All in the company of this sweet, smart, handsome human. The vast majority of people in her kingdom would be appalled, would think that a human was beneath her. Kaylah hadn't thought that way in a long time. But she couldn't deny that this could never work. She couldn't—wouldn't—abandon her kingdom, her cause. Even for someone she enjoyed, for a budding romance.

Eric's hand cautiously grazed hers. She tried to ignore the butterflies in her stomach. They'd made an appearance earlier as well, when he'd gotten the guts to hold her hand in the last twenty minutes of the movie. None of her Ivy suitors would have had the courage to move so quickly with the crown princess.

"What do you say to another date next week?" he asked.

Her heart deflated. No matter the lie—summer camp or traveling—she was always back home in the Green Lands for the summer. "I'll be out of town. I will be for the whole summer." She frowned, having intentionally skirted around that in prior conversations. She didn't get a choice in the matter, and aside from royal obligations and family expectations, she had meetings established with others to try to bring them into her cause.

"Oh." Eric slowly retracted his hand. "Really? Or did this just not go as well as I thought?"

"No! I loved tonight. Really." She raised her eyebrows, making eye contact. "My mom and I fly out to Paris in three days."

"Oh. You don't seem that excited for the most romantic place in the world."

She grinned. "I'm not going there to find romance."

He smiled in return. "Well, then… Three days?"

She nodded.

"Then I may sound like I'm desperate or something, but…" He reached out, holding her hand again. "How busy are you tomorrow? I, uh, well—we could do lunch. Start earlier and see how the day goes?"

Kaylah beamed. "I'd love that. I'm free all day." She and Ginger were really only waiting until Nuren got back to the human world.

"Great." He studied her eyes. "I should head out. How does a hug sound?"

She quickly felt at ease in his arms. Not fearing for her life. Not dreading the dating game and courtly obligations. Just being there, making a genuine connection. It didn't hurt, either, to be embracing someone with strong arms and a strong jawline.

It was the night before she was set to take off with Ginger for their home realm. Kaylah and Eric slowly walked up to her porch as she reflected on their long day together. A picnic in the park, then bowling, pizza, and capping it off with ice cream with Rachel and 'David.' Soren had returned from the Green Lands before Uncle Nuren. Rachel had given Kaylah a wink of approval after seeing the 'hunk' she'd reeled in.

Standing by the door, Kaylah turned around to face Eric, her heart hurting. She could do this all day, every day—just spending time with him. She'd always feared being unable to connect with someone this way, to have a relationship where she didn't run out of things to say.

"I really enjoyed today," he said.

She nodded, barely able to smile. "Me too."

"It was nice to meet your friends."

A more genuine smile took hold. "Yeah. Rach is great." She lifted a skeptical eyebrow. "You really liked David?"

Eric wrinkled his nose. "Maybe not my cup of tea. But perhaps he'll grow on me."

She smirked, appreciating Eric's good taste.

He set the pizza box he'd been holding down on the porch bench.

"You're sure you don't want to take that?" she asked.

He shrugged, moving closer and holding her hands. "I'm good."

"I'll probably just have one slice of cold pizza in the morning, and then my dad will eat the rest of it."

He bit his lip. "That's some pretty amazing pizza, and I suppose it wouldn't hurt my chances to have your dad eating it, as long as he associates it with me."

She playfully intertwined their fingers, looking down at them. "Hurt your chances, huh?" She looked back up, gazing into his eyes.

He frowned. "You really don't think your parents would budge on their 'no electronics' rule? That's so archaic."

Kaylah matched his frown. That was almost always the story with Rachel, too. That Ginger and Nathan were ridiculously protective of their family time on vacation—electricity and human electronics didn't function in the Green Lands. Sometimes, someone else would be tasked with sending messages to Rachel on Kaylah's behalf, but she loathed that for the lack of privacy and authenticity. "Sorry. Not gonna happen."

Eric pursed his lips. "I guess, just… Don't forget about me?"

She squeezed his hand. "I won't. I'm not going to Paris to fall for anyone."

"I really want to kiss you."

Her heart beat faster. "I really want to say yes."

He searched her face. "Is that a yes? Or a confusing way of saying no?"

Moving his hands to her waist, she smiled wider. "Come a little closer and we'll find out."

Without hesitation, his lips met hers in the sweetest, most perfect first kiss. He pulled back first, but her heart was yearning for more. "I'm going to think of you every day while I'm gone."

"Same." He swallowed. "Is it… I don't know if it's even fair to ask… Not that you have to answer right away, but do you think you'd want to be…"

She gazed into his eyes, loving the feel of his hands on her waist. "Your girlfriend?"

He grinned, confirming they were on the same wavelength. They'd only known each other for less than a week, but they'd spent the bulk of those days together.

"Yeah," he said softly.

Her cheeks were starting to hurt from all the smiling. "I'd love to."

"Great." He bent down, holding her tighter, placing a couple more tender kisses on her lips that made her forget how to breathe entirely. "I guess I should let you go so you're well rested for the airport, huh?"

She nodded. "I'll start counting the days." After a long hug, it hurt to watch him go.

With pizza box in hand, she went inside and trudged up the stairs to the kitchen. She set the box down, filling a glass of water and sipping. Leaning back, she mused on their evening, on his perfect kiss, his perfect everything.

"Interesting choice."

Her mood instantly plummeted from the clouds, as 'David' entered the kitchen.

"I don't know what you're talking about." She took another sip of water.

He raised both eyebrows. "Really? Making out with a human like that."

She narrowed her eyes. "Privacy—ever heard of it? And that was far from making out."

Soren leaned back against the kitchen counter. "But is that idiot approved? I highly doubt that. And I'm sorry if you haven't gotten the memo, but Her Highness doesn't get privacy. None of us do when we're in our own realm—why should you expect it here?"

"Why are you here, Soren?" She set her glass down. "You're an idiot to show up like this. We didn't have a scheduled meeting. What if Eric or Rachel or someone else saw you come by? How would that look?"

He gave her an insincere pouty face. "A big brother can't just drop by to check up on his little sis?"

"No. Not when you're just supposed to be a random dick that's dating my best friend."

He reached out with a vine, lifting the pizza box lid. She slapped his vine away. "Go crawl back where you came from."

"You're not even going to ask how my visit back home went?"

Kaylah rolled her eyes. "How was your visit?"

"It was great. My visits are always good."

She felt nauseous. "Enjoyed your time with some whores, then?"

He smirked. "Nope. Spent most of it with Beata."

Tilting her head to the side, Kaylah flashed a disingenuous smile. "I group her with them."

His lips puckered with rage as his vibrant green eyes turned dark. "Screw you, *Meg*."

Talking about his Ivy girlfriend like that always provoked his anger. The kind of anger that she actually feared sometimes. He knew how much Kaylah hated her fake name, and using it was all he could really do as an impotent prick who would someday be subject to the rulings of his little sister. Looking away, she grabbed the pizza box, opening the fridge door and crouching down to make room for it.

"Have you seen Teagan?" Soren asked.

Kaylah froze, her heart pounding. She fought to train her breathing as she recalled the screams, the blood, the awful noises, as Teagan, Soren's assassin buddy, had died by her hand.

"Something wrong?" Soren asked after no response on her part. His voice was innocently curious, though she knew her uncle's minion was rarely innocent.

Snapping out of her episode, she mustered a reply. "Yes, I just realized there's no way this whole box will fit in here." She stood up, closing the door and forcing a smile.

"So have you?"

"What?" she asked while opening a kitchen cupboard.

"Seen Teagan," he drawled with annoyance.

She furrowed her brow, pulling out plasticware for the pizza. "Why would I keep track of Teagan?"

Soren shrugged. "He's gone missing. Can't find him in either world. I checked when I was back there."

"Umm… That sounds less than ideal. Uncle knows?" She tried to add the sound of genuine curiosity and concern to her voice.

Soren nodded.

"I'm sure he'll figure it out. It's not like I'm here to babysit your assassin friends. I don't really give a crap about Teagan or any of the others. Maybe he got tired of working with you and chose the life of a deserter. I know I would."

Glaring, Soren inched closer. "Maybe you should care more."

She turned, challenging him with her hands on her hips. "Maybe you should use your time more wisely. Why would you even waste your time looking for him back home? What if one of Rachel's weed brothers discovered him and took him out? It sounds like you're wasting time looking in the wrong realm, idiot. And if their weed network is on to us…"

Soren studied her face. "You make a good point."

She smiled again. "I know. One of us has to have a brain, right?"

"I love our chats. Just remember, someday when you're coronated as our queen, people will be asking me what it was like growing up as the brother of the beautiful, sweet queen. I'll be able to recount your lovely sentiments about missing teenage assassins with worried parents back home. 'She told me she didn't care whether he was dead or alive. Didn't get active. Didn't try.'"

"You have plenty of your own indiscretions, don't you?" She scowled.

"People won't care as much about that, will they? By the time you become queen, I'll be a nobody." He winked and turned. "Love you. Have a good visit back home." He left out the back door.

Once the door clicked closed, she promptly bolted the lock and let out a shaky breath. Gnawing on her lip, she stared at the closed fridge, analyzing their chat. Had he just been concerned about his friend? Or did Soren know? Did he suspect? Did that mean her uncle or parents knew or suspected her?

"How was your date with that boy?" Nathan said, entering the kitchen.

Kaylah relaxed into a smile, allowing her mind to drift back to Eric. "Good."

Nathan awkwardly cleared his throat. "I imagine so, if you're kissing him."

Kaylah blushed. "I really like him." While she despised Soren's spying, Nathan's had been expected. He was paid to be her protector, her fake father.

"But—"

"I said I'd be his girlfriend." She lifted her chin slightly.

Nathan, however, tilted his head down a bit. "That wasn't the wisest move."

She frowned. "Rachel could bloom any day. You guys know I'm tired of the suitors. And it's stupid to worry about matching me up so seriously. I have a limited amount of time in this world. Just let me be happy."

Nathan sighed. "We want you to be happy. But we don't have much say in that part of things. You know that."

Looking down, she fidgeted with her hands. "Dating a human would be more convincing for my cover, anyway. You could help me convince my uncle…" She looked up after getting no response.

Nathan eyed her, pursing his lips. "Fine. We'll try."

Kaylah beamed, giving him a big hug. "Thank you!"

"You're welcome." He threw a quick glance at the pizza box. "Leftovers before leaving for home?"

"They're for you. From Eric."

He grinned, opening the box with a vine and slipping out a piece with his hand. "Smart boy."

"Did you know that Soren was coming over tonight?" she asked.

Nathan shook his head. "He dropped by asking about a friend of his."

Kaylah nodded, considering the risk she was about to take. "Are you a whisper rifter, Nathan?"

His eyes grew wide as he finished chewing. "What?"

"A whisper rifter. The way I look at it, I figure most palace guards are. Hand-picked former assassins, right?"

Nathan cleared his throat again, taking another bite. "Everyone knows they're just a—"

"Don't say myth." She crossed her arms. "I know they're real." Though she'd grown up believing the same as other Ivies, that whisper rifters were as ridiculous as Bigfoot, she now knew better. Her run-in with Teagan had cemented that truth. A truth that her own parents had kept from her, likely a secret only passed down from a paranoid queen to her heir when the time was right.

Setting down his piece of pizza, Nathan grabbed a napkin and wiped his hands. "Even if I believed or knew about such a thing, I suspect you know that I couldn't confirm it." He gently raised his eyebrows. "Not even to you, Your Highness."

Her hope deflated. "Don't 'Your Highness' me, Nathan." They only called her that when they were acting as her paid protectors, not her surrogate parents.

His face was stern, or at least as close to stern as it ever got. "Don't put me in that position."

She hesitated, unsure if she should press more. She'd need *a lot* more loyalty than this if she was going to pull everything off. "You know, you and Ginger lied to me for years about Rachel's true identity. I think you owe me."

"That was under orders. You weren't ready to keep that kind of secret, to know that truth."

She analyzed his body language, determination in the set of her jaw. "I'm ready to know this truth. And whether or not you confirm it, I think you are one. And I want to know if you've ever spied on me."

He studied her face in silence. "I've never followed you or watched you without your knowledge." His voice and posture seemed sincere.

Her anxiety grew, knowing it might be now or never, with the way things were falling into place. "Do I have your loyalty, Nathan?"

"Of course you do." He furrowed his brow. "Why would you ask that?"

"If, um…" She stood a little straighter. "Do you know what my uncle has planned for Rachel?"

Nathan gave her a sympathetic frown. "You know we're as fond of her as you are. But sweetheart, she's a Seeder. You've known for a long time that this was the plan."

Narrowing her eyes, she suspected that he didn't actually know. "You're talking about intel and death?"

"What else?"

"You don't know what they've started doing at the palace?"

Nathan shook his head, his eyes squinting. "I haven't been privy to palace information in years."

"You said I have your loyalty, but who has it more? Me or my parents?"

He tilted his head with disapproval. "You can't ask that kind of question."

Her heart was pounding, her chest tight. "But I am. And I will. Because some day you're going to have to choose."

Nathan swallowed hard, staring at her. "What is this all about? A human boy? Spies? Rachel?"

"No. It's much more than that. But I…" She took a deep breath. "You can turn me in tonight, and I can only imagine the punishment I would face, or you can help me. Those are the choices. I'm going to… I've already…"

Nathan's face was grim. "What have you done?"

Tears clouded her vision, exhaustion filling her entire being. "I need your help."

He slowly nodded. "Let's go talk this over with Ginger, okay?"

She sniffled, wiping tears away. "Yeah."

Kaylah sat cross-legged on the hotel suite bed, staring at her phone. *I need to get it over with. I shouldn't be wasting time like this.* Years of learning, planning, plotting. And now everything was set in motion. She shouldn't be taking time at the beginning of a revolution for a personal indulgence.

But she couldn't stop herself. He meant too much.

Bolstering her courage, she forced her fingers to type out the words on her new burner phone.

<Please don't say anything. I'm safe. I need to see you. In private. XO> She closed her eyes and sent it off, then waited in agony for a couple of minutes—he should have just gotten home from school.

A text chimed in. <MEG?!? Where have you been?>

She smiled, her heart filling with hope. <Yes. Are you free tomorrow?>

<Yes. All day. What's going on? You guys are back? I can meet at your place.>

<I'll explain everything. Meet me at the mall at 8 a.m.?>

Instead of getting a return text, her phone rang with an incoming call, and she answered.

"What's going on? If you want to talk in private, the mall isn't really the best place to go," he said.

She sighed. "I know this is going to sound crazy, but I need you to pretend you haven't heard from me since our breakup. No one can know we've talked. It's … dangerous."

Silence.

"Um… Okay? Do you know what happened to Rachel and David? Gosh, and Rachel's stepdad. And then you guys went missing. It's been crazy here, and your family up and goes on vacation in the middle of school?"

She frowned. "I can explain everything. I promise. But I need you to keep it a secret that we've been in touch. Call me at this number when you get to the mall?"

"Sure."

"Okay… Thank you."

It took him a moment to respond. "Yeah. I… I'm glad to hear your voice."

Her heart ached. "You too. See you tomorrow."

Kaylah made her bed and paced the hotel room all morning. A knock came on her door at 8:30 a.m. and she looked through the peephole. Beaming, she unlocked the door and ripped it open. She yanked Eric inside and threw her arms around him. He paused briefly before returning the hug—not a passionate embrace like they used to share.

She'd forgotten. They were broken up. It was all her fault.

Kaylah stepped back, and they shared an awkward half-smile. "Hey, um… sorry if that was weird to have someone else meet you there. Let's sit down."

They moved over to a small table with two chairs. "Yeah. Pretty weird." He pressed his lips together, looking her over. "What's going on?"

She gave him a hesitant smile. He looked sharp and was wearing her favorite cologne. "How are you doing? I missed you."

He looked down, shrugging. "Fine."

The distance between them gutted her. "I still love you."

He met her gaze, the hurt apparent in his eyes. "You have a funny way of showing it."

Kaylah frowned. She deserved that after breaking up with him, and not even giving an explanation. "I'm sorry. I did that to keep you safe." Even meeting with him now wasn't a great idea. And she should have broken up with him earlier, put more time and space between them; but she hadn't been able to bring herself to do it when she should have.

He sighed. "What's going on? This is dangerous? Safety? You know what's going on with Rachel and David running away? Her stepdad going missing? What do you know? Three people I cared about and three of their parents just go missing all in one week, and there wasn't even a mention about it on the news!"

She gazed into his kind eyes, her heart heavy. "Are you dating anyone?"

He raised his eyebrows. "Is that any of your business? You dumped me, remember? And I don't see how that has anything to do with the topic at hand."

She placed her hands on the table, calculating. She couldn't really tell him anything if he wasn't willing to be part of her life.

"No. I'm not dating anyone," Eric volunteered. "You're not that easy to get over."

She blushed. "A girl can hope."

He shifted in his seat. "So?"

She nodded, getting to their reason for meeting. "I reached out because… Well, like I said, you mean a lot to me. And you're one of the few people I trust, Eric. I have a lot of news, a lot of secrets."

He shrugged again. "Shoot."

Taking a deep breath, she bolstered her courage. "Let's go over the facts in phases. Rachel's stepdad, Rob. He was my uncle."

Eric's eyes widened in surprise. "What? Does Rachel know that? Wait, what?"

"My parents aren't my parents. And David's my brother."

He stared at her, blinking a few times. "Why would you say that?"

"Because it's true. It's complicated. I'll explain it."

He narrowed his eyes in apparent disbelief.

This could be going better…

"David is my older brother," she said. "I know that sounds crazy. But it's true. Rob was our uncle. And Ginger and Nathan are my guardians while I live here, but they're not my parents."

"And why would you all be pretending to be something you're not?"

She swallowed hard. "Do you believe in aliens?"

He busted out laughing. "No… Were you abducted? Is that why you're making up crazy stories? Is that where everyone went? Were the guys that interrogated me from the FBI or something?"

She smiled. "No. No aliens. It might be weirder than that." She reached forward, grasping his hands. The warmth of his large hands was reassuring, but the knots in her stomach grew for fear of his denial. She searched his face intently. "I'm not completely human. I don't want you to freak out." She extended vines from her wrists, wrapping them around their joined hands.

Eric froze on the spot, staring down at them. He finally glanced up. "What… What are you?"

She bit her lip. "Rob, David, Ginger, and Nathan are all like this. Rachel's not human either, but she's different."

He blinked, swallowing, but not saying anything.

"My people are called Ivies."

He pressed his lips together, nodding.

She frowned. "Are you freaked out?"

He went back to staring at her vines, his brow furrowed. "Um… I… don't know…"

"Well… It's a great start that you didn't run or scream…"

He shook his head, wide-eyed. "I'm not drugged, right?"

Kaylah frowned again, thinking of Rachel. "No. You're very much awake and lucid."

He kept nodding, processing. "You're not human. You're secretly related or not related to people that have gone missing. I guess I never really knew you at all."

He hadn't said it in a judgmental way, but it pierced deep. She retracted her vines. "You may not have known those sides of me, but in a lot of ways, you know me better than anyone else in my life."

Eric took a deep breath, sitting up straighter. "So, what happened? Why did everyone go missing? Is everyone okay?"

Barely able to look at him, she pinched the bridge of her nose. "There's bad news and good news about all of that. Ginger and Nathan are in hiding for the same reason I broke up with you—so no one would come after you."

"Why would someone come after us?"

"Because I'm in a tight spot. And, um … as for David and Rachel… He kidnapped her, but I got her out."

"Shit, Meg! You're not joking, are you?"

She shook her head. "You saw my vines. I think it's safe to say I'm not joking about anything today." She cleared her throat. "And my name's not Meg. It's Kaylah." She shyly added, "Most people know me as … Princess Kaylah."

He cocked his head. "I mean, why not? A princess."

She smiled. "I'm the next ruler after my mother."

He closed his eyes. "Ruling over a kingdom of plant people?"

She stifled a laugh. "Kind of. It's funny when you say it that way. We prefer 'botanical beings.'"

"Oh, well, my apologies, Your Highness." He raised his hands.

She got more serious. "You can call me Meg if you'd like. Though, I do prefer Kaylah."

He nodded guiltily. "Is Rachel okay? When did you help her? She hasn't been back to school."

"She won't be able to come back. She's back home with her people."

"Right. You said she's different? And that covers everyone but her stepdad."

Kaylah wrung her hands. "Right. Yes. And Rob won't be coming back, because he's dead."

Eric's eyes widened in shock. "Seriously?" he whispered.

"My people have been at war with Rachel's for a long time … like … a couple of centuries." Kaylah reached out to hold his hands. "How freaked out are you right now? Be honest."

He waited a moment to answer. "I don't even know what to think."

How much could she throw at him in one go? How much could he handle of the truth, period? "I still love you. Do you think you could ever love me again?"

Looking down, he fought a frown. "I never *stopped* loving you."

She knew she should feel hope, even relief. She didn't. "Even now? Now that you know this crazy part of me?"

He took a painfully long amount of time to reply. "I have a million questions. But … I miss you. I miss us."

She nodded. That might be the best she could get. "It gets worse."

He raised an eyebrow. "Worse than kidnapping and Rob dying in a war?"

She rubbed his hands with her thumbs. If she was going to do this, she needed to be completely honest with Eric. "My people have been on the wrong side of the war. We're not innocent. Rob and David are horrible people. I'm the one that killed Rob."

He snapped his hands back from her grip. "You what?!"

Her heart sank. "They were torturing her, Eric! And other girls just like her. The world is a better place without him."

"Maybe…" He narrowed his eyes. "Are you sure you're the one that gets to make that call? Who lives and who freakin' dies? You murdered someone, Meg!"

She clenched her teeth. "I know! My own uncle. But he has countless lives on his head. War is ugly, Eric. I'm sorry if you don't understand that, living here in the cozy human world, in a nation at peace."

He ran his hands through his hair. "What else? Why do I feel like this conversation is never going to end?"

She was already chin-deep, might as well go all the way. "I will never apologize for executing an evil man. But I will always feel guilty for playing a part in Rachel's kidnapping."

His jaw dropped in disgust. "You're kidding me. She's your best friend!" He shook his head. "I think I've heard enough." He stood up and walked toward the door.

Kaylah hopped up and blocked his exit. "Please. Hear me out."

"You just told me I knew you better than anyone else. *This* isn't the Meg I knew."

Grimacing, she fought back tears. "I never wanted to hurt her. And I got her back. And I'm... I've turned on my family, my people." She reached to hold his hand, and he jerked it back. She hung her head in shame. "Hear me out. If you still hate me when we're done talking, I'll leave you alone."

He scowled. "What if I want to leave right now? Will you kill me? Or kidnap me? Or who knows what else you've done to people?"

Willing to beg, plead, do anything, she looked into his eyes. "I need you in my life. I would never hurt you. And I've never hurt anyone unless I had to. Rachel included."

He rubbed his forehead. "Why are you even telling me any of this?"

"I told you. I love you. I miss you. And I need you to know the truth."

Pursing his lips, he tilted his head to the side. "So, the truth... Your family is messed up. You're a princess plant-person thing... There's a war. You helped kidnap your best friend, killed your uncle, and lied to me about everything. Did I miss anything?"

Kaylah sighed. "Yes. The most important parts. Rachel's safe and alive because of me, despite what I had to do. You can't grant forgiveness on her behalf, Eric. I can only hope she gives me that when I meet with her next. And I'm hoping that'll be soon. I would be convicted of treason for what I'm doing. I'm leading a revolution. I'm coordinating people to fight back. To end the war, the oppression, the death. If you believe everything I've told you so far, then believe me now when I say I'm doing my best to fix things. I'm planning on approaching the leaders of Rachel's people to try and form an alliance."

He studied her face, still visibly skeptical and upset. "You said you're the next ruler. That means a queen, right? You're saying none of your actions were your fault. Last I checked, the pawn and the queen have very different places on a chessboard."

A faint smile grew on her face. "I appreciate that you understand the difference." Her shoulders dropped. "I've spent a little too much time playing the pawn, and not enough time preparing to rule."

He let out a heavy sigh, walking back to his seat. "I want to hear everything. Start to finish. Don't leave anything out."

She finally allowed herself to hope, joining him at the table.

A good hour later, Kaylah had given Eric a thorough explanation of the Green Lands and details of the nations at war.

He frowned, reaching out his hands. "So, I can't join you there?"

She shook her head. "But I can visit. And maybe, someday… I don't know. I have dreams. But they don't mean much if I'm dead. Right now, my family would do anything to find out where I am. That includes hurting you and other people to get to me. You need to swear to me you won't talk about any of this to others."

Eric smiled. "Wouldn't even if I wanted to. I'd rather not sound crazy."

She chuckled before settling on a look of admiration. "You're amazing."

"How can I help?"

Her heart melted. "You're the best. Do you know that?"

He grinned. "I fell for a pretty ambitious girl. And I know I'm no soldier, but there's got to be something I can do."

She rubbed the back of his hands with her thumbs. "Actually, there is. That is … if you're willing to move a couple of hours away as soon as graduation is over."

"Name it."

She raised an eyebrow. "Really?"

"Yes."

There were a few things he could do to help Unitas, while staying out of harm's way. "I'm setting up safe houses for meetings and defectors joining the cause. I can't promise it will be completely safe, but—"

"Consider it done."

She cocked her head to the side. "I love you."

He read her face. "You might have said that already. A time or two, or twenty." He winked. "And I love you, too."

She glanced past him to the bed. "How do you feel about cuddling and chatting? You said you have all day free?"

He looked back and then met her eyes. "Cuddle? Is that why you invited me to meet you in a hotel room?" He smirked.

"Hey! I'm meeting you here because it's a safe place out of the public eye." She blushed, then stood up. "Let's start with a hug. I've been needing one of those."

He got up and pulled her in for a tight embrace. "I'm most definitely good with cuddling." He scooted them a few feet to the edge of the bed. "Tiiiiiimber!" He flopped over on the bed with her still in his arms.

Kaylah giggled, snuggling up to him. She couldn't help herself, gazing lovingly at his sweet face. She shifted and gave him a couple of tender kisses. The spark was still there. Eric moved his hand up to the side of her face, leaning over and laying a passionate kiss on her that sent her heart racing.

They'd talked about prom night being their first time together, despite how cliché it was. They'd missed their chance because her focus on Unitas had driven a wedge between them. She didn't want to miss this chance now.

"I leave in the morning." She studied his face, desperation in her eyes. "I… I wish you could go with me. And I wish you could stay the night."

He gave a soft grin. "I wish I could, too. Would be mighty hard explaining to my parents why I didn't come home tonight." He moved closer, caressing her neck with his lips. "But I don't have anything else planned for today. How long is it going to take to discuss this safe house business?"

She smirked. "Not all day."

Kaylah sat impatiently in an Ivy pub smuggler's room—a small back room with a table, chairs, and storage. She shook her head. *This is what my life is reduced to. No palace. No human graduation.* She cursed the timing of Rachel's bloom cutting things short, though she knew that was hardly fair.

The internal door opened, and she gave a forced smile as Guillen joined her.

"Hey. Glad to see you all in one piece," he said.

She let out a long sigh. "You too."

He sat down opposite her. "You certainly *sound* happy to see me."

She cocked her head to the side. "I'm just trying to figure out why you and I are having this debriefing instead of Jon and I…" She raised her eyebrows.

Guillen raised an eyebrow in return. "He checked in, right? He's okay?"

"Yes. But why are you and I having this meeting instead of him coming to see me? What happened?"

Guillen rubbed at a scratch on the edge of the table. "I volunteered to stay back."

Kaylah was unamused. "You both had orders. Why did you not follow them as directed?"

He shrugged. "It wasn't a huge thing. She got home safe. We got home safe."

Kaylah leaned forward. "You were to be the one that left first. Why did you volunteer to hang back? That was reckless."

He scowled. "I was fine."

"Dammit, Guillen. That's not your call to make! We put a huge arrow pointing to those woods so they'd find her. What would have happened if they'd stumbled upon you?"

"It didn't happen."

"It could have."

He leaned back. "We're going to go there? You of all people? You're going to cite my 'disability'? Why did you ask me to take on the mission if you didn't think I was capable of doing my part?"

She shook her head. "I'll bring up your limitations when they're relevant, yes." She furrowed her brow. He was a proud man and she'd always liked that, but he was never defiant like this. "We use our resources wisely. We play to our strengths. You did your part. She got home safe. It was Jon's part to ensure she was picked up by the right people, and then rift out."

He stared at her for a moment. "It was a risk I was willing to take."

She narrowed her eyes. "Did he ask you to stay?"

"No."

She put a fist to her forehead. "I get that our relationship is different. But you need to look past that and obey my orders. This is serious."

He glared. "I'm pretty sure I understood how serious this was the first time we killed someone. Don't patronize me."

"Then help me understand. It was a simple order. You're one of my best spies. I can't have you taking unnecessary risks." She studied his face. *Why would he put himself in harm's way?* He was usually so organized, so meticulous, so diligent.

He threw his hands up. "I don't know what you want me to say. I just … needed to know she was okay." He averted his gaze.

Then it clicked. Kaylah studied him, a smile forming on her face. "You like her."

Guillen quickly glanced up, then looked back down. "You know me so well. I risked my life and traipsed around the Green Lands to take advantage of a traumatized teenage girl."

That broke Kaylah's heart. "How is she?"

Guillen rubbed his hands together. "I don't know. She had some ups and downs. Some pretty intense nightmares. She's ... going to struggle for a while." He met Kaylah's gaze. "You haven't seen her yet?"

Kaylah shook her head. "They haven't reached out yet. If it gets too late in the season, I'll have to consider my backup plans. And they're a heck of a lot trickier..." She reached her hand out on the table. "She's pretty. And nice, isn't she?"

He grinned. "Don't you think she's a little young for me?"

Kaylah shrugged. "Five and a half years isn't *that* big of a deal. After Soren, I have a feeling she'd appreciate a more mature man."

Guillen rolled his eyes. "Yeah, well, you weren't the one that had people thinking he was some kind of a perv by taking his kid cousin out into the woods."

That was hard to hear. No doubt Soren had bullied him about it on one of Guillen's visits to the palace. "If they had ever really thought that, we wouldn't have been allowed to slip away for training like we did."

He smiled. "I don't know if she realized how much older I am. She called me a ... Boy Scout?"

Kaylah gave him a soft smile in return. Soren took every chance he could to mock Guillen for his lack of human-world knowledge. Kaylah had always found it endearing. And she appreciated that he felt safe enough to be vulnerable with her about that kind of thing. "A 'Boy Scout' just means she thinks you're capable. It's not necessarily referencing your age. Take it as a compliment."

His smile subtly widened. "Anyway. What else did you need to know from me? She's back home with her family like she should be. Jon and I moved on safely."

"I want to hear more about your time with her. Do you think she'd be up for helping? I don't know how much training she was able to do with my poisoning. Or how much she hates me…"

He shook his head. "I think she understands what you had to do." His cheeks turned pink. "She's pretty talented and smart. And she seems to want to help."

Kaylah smiled at seeing him blush. Guillen was always so private about his life, and love life.

He picked at his fingernails. "You should, uh, ask her about Seeders like me next time you see her. She was going to look into it."

She grinned wider. "She knows?"

"Yeah." He looked at a clock on the wall. "I should get going. Do you have anything to add to my standing orders?"

"No. Do what you're doing. I'll reach out."

Guillen stood. "Great. Stay safe."

Kaylah got up and gave him a hug. "You too, love you."

"You too."

She sat back down at the table; she'd be having a late dinner served soon.

Guillen lingered, looking down at the table. He knocked his knuckles on the wood. "When you, uh, see her… Tell her hi from me."

Kaylah smirked. "I most certainly will."

He met her eyes, unable to hold back a shy grin of his own. "See you later."

To Love a Monster:
A Villain's Love Story

Prince Soren had been attending upper-class youth gatherings for the last year. No matter your station, the invite was only extended on your fourteenth birthday. It was a nice diversion, providing more entertainment and variety than he usually got at the palace and touring around with his parents.

On a beautiful summer's eve, he sat playing cards at just such a gathering with a couple of his friends and a few beautiful girls. The boys were sharp, the girls charming in dresses fitted to accentuate their features as they matured.

Live music played somewhere down the hall, colliding with the chatter of teens from various rooms in the manor.

"That's me again," a friend to Soren's right announced, laying down another winning hand. The young man beamed with arrogance.

Soren huffed. He'd been close to winning. Maybe not *that* close, but if he'd had another turn or two, he could have turned it to his advantage. "Another round."

His friend shrugged. "If you'd like. But you'll have to wait a minute." He headed toward the restroom while the dealer shuffled.

When the hands were dealt, Soren grinned. The players were busy looking at their hands, though the observers that had gathered around watched mostly Soren. He was used to that. Being the eldest child of the queen and king had its perks, even if he wasn't the widely adored heir his little sister was.

Still holding his hand, Soren poked out a vine and peeked at what his absent neighbor had been dealt. *Not bad.* He set his own cards down and picked up the others.

"Soren!" another friend chastised.

Soren laughed. "Teaching the bastard a lesson. I think it's perfectly fair." He plucked out his friend's best cards and swapped them for his worst, just in time for him to return to the room.

Everyone remained hushed about the exchange as play resumed. Like the others, a cute young girl sitting across from Soren had her eyes focused on him, but hers were narrowed, dancing between the two young men. When Soren took his first turn, the girl rolled her eyes, setting down her hand.

"I think I'm done playing for now," she announced, standing up.

Soren stroked his cards as she walked away. Her jet-black hair was perfectly styled to frame her face, and she wore a powder-blue dress. He leaned over to the friend he'd cheated from. "Who was that girl?"

"That one? Beata Remsgard. I think this is her second invite."

Soren stole another glance as she mingled with some girls at the end of the room. "Remsgard?"

"Yeah. Those are her older sisters over there. Their father is over the reject communities."

"Ah, gotcha." It now clicked for Soren. She was as beautiful and as slim as any of the other girls. Not as many curves, but if she was only fourteen, she had time to catch up. But that look she'd given him—rolling her eyes. It bothered him.

Shaking off his distraction, Soren won the round. He even won the next round without cheating. As the dealer shuffled again, Beata exited the room. Soren stood. "I've had enough for now." He followed her out into the hallway. It was dimly lit with only a handful of people chatting yards away.

"Beata, right?"

She turned, curtsying. "Yes, Your Highness."

He approached her, clasping his hands in front of him. "You left the game abruptly."

She shrugged, giving him a courtesy smile.

"You don't approve of the way I played?"

"Does His Highness want the truth?"

"Yes."

She cocked her head. "I didn't find it particularly amusing."

He grinned. "Why? He won plenty. I was just having some fun."

Beata scanned his face with confidence. "I'd expect more from a member of the royal family."

He glared. *How dare she judge me? She's barely important enough to be invited to these parties!* "You don't think the royal family should be able to take what they want? That's a bold political stance to be sharing."

A pair of giggling girls down the hallway distracted her for a moment before she turned her focus back to Soren. "On the contrary. The royal family should know what's best for our kingdom and act to obtain it. Dissenters would call it theft. But it still requires work and ambition to take what you want."

He smiled. "So, you agree with the palace agenda, but you think something as small as a little … sleight of hand … in a game of cards is too wicked?"

"It's petty. Beneath you."

He furrowed his brow. "You certainly share harsh criticism openly."

She pursed her lips, not shrinking from his authority or disapproval. "His Highness said he wanted me to speak the truth. I can change to agreeing with you if you'd like."

He drew a deep breath, shaking his head. "No. I like you. You've got spunk."

She smirked.

"What about a king? Does he get more leverage in your eyes than a prince?"

She busted out laughing before raising a hand to muffle it.

Soren clenched his jaw.

"I'm so sorry." She bit her lip. "I just… You'll never be king, unless you're planning on marrying your younger sister." She raised her eyebrows. "I know it's happened in human history, but that would be a *shocking* choice for the Ivy royal family."

"No." He scowled. "I don't plan on marrying my sister." He turned to walk away.

"My apologies, Your Highness." Her voice was softer. "I meant no offense."

He faced her. "I'm not used to being mocked." His ears were warm. He didn't know what to make of her. The confidence was refreshing, the condescension—not so much.

She gave a gentle nod, frowning. "Please forgive me. You're handsome, well-educated, and well-liked. I'm not used to speaking with anyone in the royal family."

His shoulders relaxed. "I guess it doesn't really matter. Sounds like you'd enjoy being with one of those other guys out there, anyway. Why would I waste my time caring about your opinions?"

She blushed. "I didn't realize we were talking about being *with* anyone… I just thought this was a regular conversation."

He cleared his throat, looking her over. "Are you dating anyone?"

She was slow to answer. "No."

"Good." He bridged the gap and slid his hands up to the nape of her neck. They locked eyes, and he pushed her back against the wall, leaning in for a kiss. Not a complete stranger to stealing a kiss from a pretty face when he wanted, he started with a couple of small, short caresses to see how she responded. She didn't resist, so he asserted himself more. He was surprised when she reciprocated.

A couple of boys rounded the corner, laughing. "Soren, you'll never believe—"

"Oh. Never mind." They retraced their steps toward the main gathering.

Soren leaned back, scanning Beata's face. She gazed into his eyes, her cheeks red.

"I like you," he said. He leaned forward, pressing himself against her and whispering into her ear. "You said the royal family should take what they want. What if I take what I want from you?" There had to be an empty room nearby. He kissed her on the neck. When she didn't respond, he stepped back to look at her.

She averted her gaze, swallowing. "I, uh… I think *some* things are best savored when you know someone a little more."

He smiled. "You've never been with anyone, have you?"

She met his eyes shyly. "I find that an impertinent question, Your Highness."

"Call me Soren."

"Soren." She fidgeted with her hands. "I could hardly ask you that kind of question in reciprocation."

He smirked. "You haven't been."

Beata opened her mouth, but nothing came out for a moment. "No."

He drew closer again, calculating. "Good. Keep it that way."

She scrunched her eyebrows. "You may have some say, someday, in how the *stunts* handle their lives and bodies. But you don't get to tell me what to do with mine."

He found her defiance—in contrast to her acceptance of his previous advances—both frustrating and perplexing. "Maybe I'm just giving you a heads-up about my intentions and desires. That's all."

She read his face with narrowed eyes and a smile. "I will amount to more than a mere slut or mistress to a prince."

His hands glided along the silky fabric of her dress, resting on her lower back. "I don't think I could ever do that to a girl like you." His eyes softened. "Sharing honestly, would you want to date me? I'd like to call on you."

She didn't take long to think it over, reaching out and playing with a button on his shirt. "Yes."

He stole another quick kiss. "Then I will. Soon." He glanced down at her chest. "Wear something more revealing."

She gave a coy grin. "I'll see what I can do."

The rest of the evening, they caught each other's eyes across the room. It drove Soren crazy. She wasn't like the other girls he'd met at these parties. She was confident, but shy. Accepting, yet critical. Passionate, but hesitant. He wanted her. More than any girl he'd wanted before.

On his way home to the palace, Prince Soren replayed their interaction. Beata had known it wasn't appropriate to ask if he'd been with anyone, and he was grateful for that. He hadn't. He might have a reputation with his peers for being a flirt and taking a girl for a little feel-up and make-out, but he hadn't taken one to bed—yet. The prospect of his first experience being with this cute, defiant girl was enticing. But it was also horrifying.

He was a prince. He needed to appear worthy of admiration, not like an awkward, bumbling idiot.

After arriving at his chambers, he loosened his collar. Pacing his room, Soren looked at his bed and made a decision.

He opened his outer door; his personal servant was standing ready, on duty.

"Do we have any servant girls my age?" Soren asked.

The man furrowed his brow. "Yes. I believe so."

Soren nodded in thought. "Bring me one."

The man's eyes widened. "Um… Your Highness? *Here?*"

Soren crossed his arms, meeting the man's challenge. "Obviously. The prettiest one. My age, or maybe a year or two younger."

The man glanced down. "Your Highness. Your parents would not approve."

"I don't give a shit! And they better not hear of it." He looked the man over; he was relatively new to this position. "Who do you think they would believe? Do you know what happened to your predecessor?"

The man gulped. "I… I'm not completely sure."

Soren sneered. He'd grown tired of the last one and his insistence on following all of the queen and king's rules. It was simple enough to plant 'stolen' palace items in the servant's quarters and have him sent off to prison. "Pray you never find out the truth about what *really* happened to him."

The man looked terrified. "Your Highness… What would I even say? The kitchen staff is going to ask me why I'm calling a girl away. What if she doesn't come willingly?"

Soren's anger peaked. "I don't give a damn about the details. That's your job. Have a nurse dose her so she doesn't throw a fit. I don't really care!"

The man's breathing became rapid, his eyes darting at the floor before him. "Yes, Your Highness." He left down the corridor, and Soren mentally prepared himself for his first time.

Beata was back home, waiting on a servant from her sister's room to help ready her for bed. Her mind was lost in thought, focused on the dashing prince. She'd heard he was passionate. That he had a temper. That he had gorgeous brown locks and bright green eyes that melted girls to his whim. He was all that and more. *And that kiss…*

Her older sister entered the room. "Callie Bremshaw said you were found in the hallway with the prince?" Her tone and expression were disapproving.

Beata grinned as the servant removed her necklace. "I won't deny it."

Her sister cocked her head. "Not a great idea, Beata. You're young."

Beata rolled her eyes. "And he's just a year older. It's not a big deal."

"Yes, but you're going to those parties to meet a *variety* of people. Not to be tainted as his plaything from an early age! He will just toss you to the side when he gets bored."

Beata gritted her teeth. "It wasn't like that. It won't be like that. We were quite frank with each other. He wants to date me."

Her sister sighed. "Just … be careful. Normal girls don't have to be so careful with normal guys. He's the prince, for goodness' sakes. And Mom and Dad aren't in a great position for *any* of us kids to get a reputation."

Beata's annoyance grew. "I'll be careful." She fought a smile, thinking of Soren fondly. "People misunderstand him."

Her sister stood with hands on hips. "Swapping slobber in a dimly lit hallway during a party means you understand him better than the rest of the realm?"

Beata chuckled. "Yes." She didn't care what her sister thought. She was enamored with him already. Those eyes, that kiss. His absolute confidence.

Her sister's voice softened. "I love you. I just think you're a bit young to play with fire."

Beata picked up her hairbrush, a warm smile forming on her lips. They hadn't even gone on their first date. And she didn't share the same qualms as her sister. "I know what I'm doing."

Bonus Material

Seeder Naming Conventions

<u>Surnames / Family Names / Last Names</u>

Children take on the first name of their mother with a gender designator added to the end ('sdotter' or 'son').

e.g. Mother's first name: Murial

Daughter: Dahlia Murialsdotter

Son: Kyle Murialson

After marriage, both parties retain the same family names they were assigned at birth (neither spouse changes their last name; they still retain their mother's name plus 'sdotter' or 'son').

Informal last names for spouses: Your spouse's first name plus 'spo.'

e.g. Wife & Husband, Murial (daughter of River) & Thod (son of Tuli)

Formal: Murial Riversdotter   Informal: Murial Thodspo

Formal: Thod Tulison   Informal: Thod Murialspo

Informal last names are used primarily to communicate familial relationships where confusion may arise.

<u>Given Names / First Names</u>

Boys are generally given human names, partially in preparation for the possibility they may be chosen to protect their sisters in the human world, and partially because their mothers were all raised in and influenced by the human world.

Girls are given names by their human hosts. While Seeder names are usually assigned around the time of their sprouting, the girls are typically given those names sometime after they bloom, after their powers come in, or upon their return to the Green Lands. Names can be rather fluid, as some may not choose to accept a new Seeder given name or surname until later in life, often due to an important event such as marriage. Each village generally has a theme for given names. Many are floral, but others vary a lot based on the terrain. Those near the Grand Sea, for example, tend to have more aquatic names.

Ivy Naming Conventions

<u>Surnames / Family Names / Last Names</u>

Women pass their last name to their husband and children. Some names or types of names can be common, the trends varying based on ancient clans they descend from.

<u>Given Names / First Names</u>

Names can vary greatly, often influenced by nature or a passed family member's name. Many are given more human names either by fathers who were assassins, or in hopes the boys would be deployed to the human world as assassins.

---

*The above are for the general population. Those in the royal family follow different surname guidelines.

<u>Royalty Rules</u>

The current ruling family's surname: Elonta. Who may bear the Elonta name: The queen and her five downline heirs. The men married to or sons born to an heir of the Mother Vines (the current queen and her five downline heirs.)

Despite the usual matriarchal name being passed to husbands, if a man bears the name of Elonta as a son to an heir, he does not change his name to match his wife's. Their children would still take their mother's last name.

Women born of the Elonta line who are not within the five-downline-heir line may not bear the name of Elonta. They are assigned the last name of Elanna. If they move up the line of heirs, becoming one of the five (due to death or abdication of heirs above them), then the last name is changed to Elonta at that time. Their husband and sons' names follow the wife/mother's.

Should an heir bearing the Elonta name abdicate or be pushed outside of the five (due to births of more heirs above them), they do not lose the Elonta name.

Ivy Royal Titles

*Downline heir means one of the five women below the current queen in the bloodline.

The Queen: Her Majesty, the high ruler.

The King: His Majesty, the queen's spouse/consort.

Princess: Her Highness, daughter to the current queen. If a sister or niece higher in the royal line becomes queen, the princess then lowers to the title of **Lady**. **Crown Princess** is the immediate heir if the current queen has more than one daughter. If the queen has only one daughter, she is the de facto Crown Princess.

Prince: His Highness, son to the current queen. Once his mother is no longer queen (by death or abdication), he becomes an **Earl**.

Lady: As noted above, previous princesses, as well as other downline heirs (the first five in succession after the current queen.)

Sir: Husbands and sons to downline heirs.

Madam: Daughters to downline heirs, who are not themselves heirs. (Those bearing the last name Elanna.)

Queen-in-waiting & King-in-waiting: The next ruler(s) before their coronation once the change has been announced and is imminent. (Due to death or abdication of the previous queen.)

*If an heir abdicates before taking the throne, they retain their current title. If a queen abdicates after she has served the kingdom, her title becomes **Matron** at the succession, and she is addressed as Her Highness.

Duke/Duchess: An earned title given by the queen herself, His or Her Grace. Their title does not automatically extend to a spouse.

*As the power of the Mother Vines resides with the queen and her downline heirs, they cannot be stripped of their titles. All others may be stripped of their titles with cause at the queen's discretion.

*Stunts may not bear royal titles.

Pronunciation Guide

(Books 1–4)

People

Beata: bay-AH-tuh

Boman/Bomen: BOW-man

Camry: CAM-ree

Dahlia: DAH-lee-uh

Eleana: el-ee-AH-nuh

    (**Leah:** LEE-uh)

Elonta: ee-LAWN-tuh

Guillen: GUY-en

Kaylah: KAY-luh

Kyas: KAI-us

Lyza: LIZ-uh

Magda: MAWG-duh

Marigold: MARE-ih-gold

    (**Mari:** mah-ree)

Murial: MYUR-ee-ul

Nuren: NYUR-en

Rian: ree-ann

Saffrona: suh-FRONE-uh

    (**Saff:** saff)

Sanath: SAN-uth

Teagan: TEE-gun

Thod: thawed

Tobias: toe-BYE-us

    (**Toby:** TOE-bee)

Places & Things

Arcadia: are-KAY-dee-uh

Boloru: bowl-OR-oo

Cassa: CASS-uh

Domiten: dome-IDE-en

Fortinda: for-TIN-da

Guenjalis: gwen-YAWL-iss

Selen: SELL-en

Siqendra: sick-EN-druh

Tonoru: TONE-oh-roo

Unitas: OO-knee-tas

*To hear an audio clip by the author, go to JHouserWrites.com/swpronunciation

 ~Please consider leaving a review!~

On Amazon, Goodreads, and/or anywhere else this book can be found.

This goes a long way to support authors!

Don't forget to sign up for J. Houser's newsletter for publishing updates, promotions, and bonus content!

JHouserWrites.com

Also, connect with the author here: YouTube, TikTok, Facebook, Instagram, and Twitter under: JHouserWrites

Seeder Wars Trilogy

Companion books in this series/world:

Upcoming titles to be announced.